STAR WARS™

MEET THE HEROES

R2-D2

STAR WARS™

MEET THE HEROES

R2-D2

Written by
Emma Grange

What language does R2-D2 speak?

What was R2-D2's bravest mission?

Does R2-D2 ever run out of power?

How does R2-D2 defend himself?

Can R2-D2 swim?

Find out the answers to these questions and many more inside!

Who is R2-D2?

A friendly droid.

Droids are machines that are **built** and **programmed** to work for others. R2-D2, also known as **"Artoo"** is **happy to help** people!

Are there other droids like R2-D2?

Yes! R2-D2 is an **"R2"** unit. All droids are given **numbers** to identify them. These numbers are a bit like **names.** Here are some others!

R4-G9

What sort of droid is R2?

An astromech droid.

These droids are built for use in **space.** They work on starships, where they **fix** controls, **target** enemies, and use mathematical calculations to help the pilot.

R4-P44   R5-D4   R4-P17

Where does R2-D2 come from?

A factory named Industrial Automaton. Droids are all built to behave the same. R2-D2 is different. He has developed **his own personality.**

Interrogation droid

Labor droid

Who uses droids?

Everybody! There are lots of jobs across the galaxy that only droids can do. The **evil Empire** uses droids. The **rebels** use droids to **fight the Empire!**

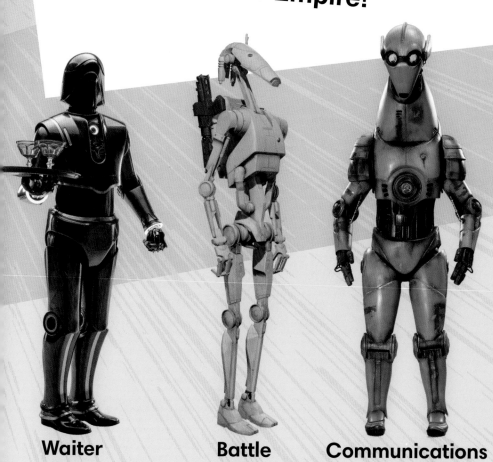

Waiter
droid

Battle
droid

Communications
droid

How big is R2-D2?

Not very big. He is just under one meter (3 feet 3 inches) tall. Here he is with young **Anakin Skywalker,** one of his many friends.

What tools does R2-D2 use?

Lots! Droids are fitted with clever **technology** and **gadgets.** Inside his metal body R2-D2 hides a **welder,** a circular **saw,** and many other useful tools.

Periscope

Grasper arm

Feet with
wheels

11

Can R2-D2 fly?

Yes! R2-D2 has **powerful rocket boosters!** The jets provide enough power for him to soar **above the ground.** This way he can travel to places his legs cannot reach.

Does R2-D2 fly starfighters?

Sometimes! R2-D2 helps navigate starfighters through space. However, his main job is to **repair** any **damage** to the ships. He also acts as **copilot,** working with whoever is in the cockpit.

Naboo starfighter

Which ships has R2-D2 flown?

Lots! R2-D2 has flown **famous rebel ships** such as **X-wings** and **Y-wings.** He has helped his Jedi friends Yoda and Anakin in their speedy **interceptors.** You can also spot him in a **shiny yellow** Naboo starfighter!

Jedi interceptor

X-wing

Y-wing

Who has owned R2-D2?

Lots of people. R2-D2 has served two royals, **Queen Amidala** and her daughter, **Princess Leia.** He has worked for **Jedi Anakin Skywalker** and his son, **Luke Skywalker.**

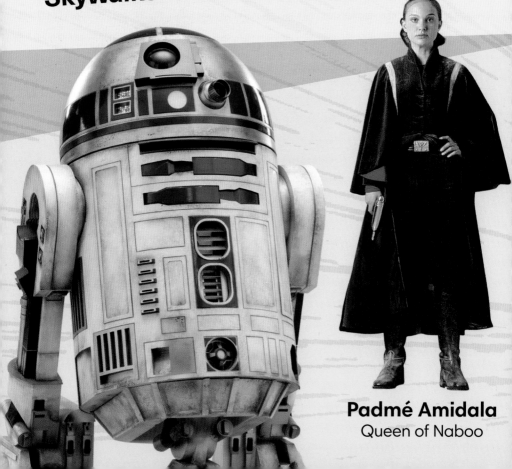

Padmé Amidala
Queen of Naboo

**Luke
Skywalker**
Jedi

Leia Organa
Princess of
Alderaan

**Anakin
Skywalker**
Jedi

Who are R2-D2's friends?

He has many. R2-D2 meets amazing friends all over the galaxy. Some of his friends are humans like **Luke Skywalker.** Some are **aliens** like **Chewbacca.**

Princess Leia
Human

Luke Skywalk
Human

Does R2-D2 have other droid friends?

Of course! R2-D2 has many droid friends. They include the ball-shaped droid **BB-8,** and the golden droid **C-3PO.**

Chewbacca
Wookiee

BB-8
Astromech droid

C-3PO
Protocol droid

19

What language does R2-D2 speak?

Binary. This is a special language used by computers. R2-D2 speaks using **beeps** and **whistles.** He understands many more languages, too.

How long can R2-D2 remember things?

Forever! Some droids get their memories wiped to make sure they forget **secrets.** However, R2-D2 has **never** had his memory wiped.

Who can understand R2-D2?

His closest friends can.

Others can tell from his tone when he is **happy** or **telling a joke.** He uses loud noises or jumps up and down to let his enemies know if he is **angry!**

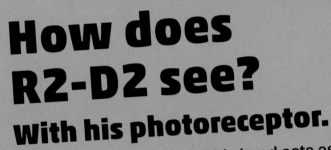

How does R2-D2 see?

With his photoreceptor.

The circle in the center of his head acts as his **eye,** also known as a photoreceptor. His head **swivels** all the way around so that he can see in **all directions!** He also has extra **scanners** and **periscopes.**

Photoreceptor

Where does R2-D2 meet C-3PO?

On the planet Tatooine. C-3PO is a **protocol droid** built by young **Anakin Skywalker.** Anakin is very good at fixing machines, vehicles, and droids. C-3PO often needs to be fixed!

Are R2-D2 and C-3PO best friends?

Yes! R2-D2 and C-3PO have been on many **adventures** together. They **understand** each other and can often be heard talking to each other. Sometimes they **tease** each other, too.

Does C-3PO always believe R2-D2?

No! R2-D2 often **surprises** C-3PO. On one trip, C-3PO thinks that R2-D2 will not be able to fix the equipment onboard the ship *Millennium Falcon*, but he's wrong. Silly C-3PO!

25

Yavin 4

Naboo

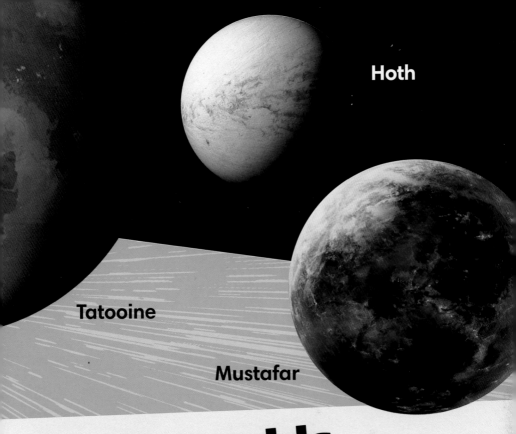

Hoth

Tatooine

Mustafar

Which worlds has R2-D2 visited?

It's impossible to count! R2-D2 travels wherever his owners ask him to go. He has visited **fiery** planets full of lava, such as Mustafar, and **beautiful** worlds of fields and seas, such as Naboo! He can often be found at a rebel base, such as the one on Yavin 4.

How does R2-D2 get his friends out of trouble?

By always being there! When his royal friend **Padmé** falls into a moving vat that is about to be filled with melted metal, R2-D2 is there to rescue her. He **switches off** the machine just in time!

Can R2-D2 hack enemy systems?

Yes. R2-D2's **technical skills** help his friends plan their missions. He assists in a rescue mission against their enemy General Grievous. By projecting an image of Grievous's ship, the *Invisible Hand*, R2-D2 is able to show all the **escape routes.**

Has R2-D2 ever been to a wedding?

Yes! R2-D2 once worked for Jedi Anakin Skywalker. Jedi are not allowed to get married. When Anakin married Padmé Amidala at a secret ceremony, R2-D2 and C-3PO were the **only guests!**

What battles has R2-D2 been in?

Many. A battlefield is **no place** for an **astromech droid,** but R2-D2 is friends with people who often **get into trouble!**

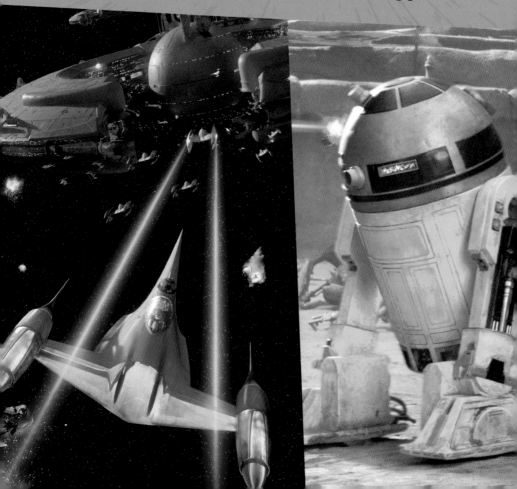

Where was R2-D2 in the Battle of Geonosis?

Fixing C-3PO! R2-D2's clumsy friend is always getting into **scrapes.** Luckily R2-D2 is on hand to put his broken friend back together again. He must **work fast** and avoid enemy **battle droids.**

How does R2-D2 escape danger?

By using clever tricks! In one fight he lets off a **cloud of smoke** to hide himself and his friends. Their stormtrooper foes **cannot see** through the thick smoke, so everyone is able to escape!

How does he distract his foes?

With loud noises and bright lights! He lets out high-pitched **whistles** and crackling, flashing **lights.** This causes a **distraction** that helps R2-D2's Jedi friends escape. Their foes do not like the noises!

How does R2-D2 defend himself?

With slippery oil! When he is caught by **super battle droids,** R2-D2 doesn't use his sharp tools. Instead, he releases **black oil** from his metal body. The oil is **slippery,** making the bigger droid drop him!

Is he useful in a fight?

Yes. R2-D2 is good at **multitasking.** While helping to fly Anakin's starfighter, R2-D2 fights off a **buzz droid** attack at the **same time!** The buzz droids have scary **saws** and **pincers!**

Can R2-D2 beat bigger droids?

Yes! R2-D2 knows that **size doesn't matter.** He may be small but he is **smart** and has more brain power than bigger droids!

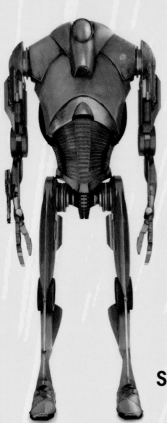

Super battle droid

How does R2-D2 save a queen?

By showing great bravery. During a battle above the planet Naboo, Queen Amidala's starship becomes damaged. R2-D2 is the **only droid** able to fix the damage. He must dodge enemy fire **at the same time!**

Does R2-D2 work for the Rebellion?

He does! Some droids are programmed to be bad. But R2-D2 works for **rebels.** The rebels want to stop the Empire from controlling the galaxy. **Loyal** R2-D2 never abandons his friends on their dangerous missions.

What was R2-D2's bravest mission?

R2-D2 goes on lots of missions.

He is very trustworthy. Rebel Princess Leia once gave him a vital **message** to **keep safe.** He had to act in secret and transport the message.

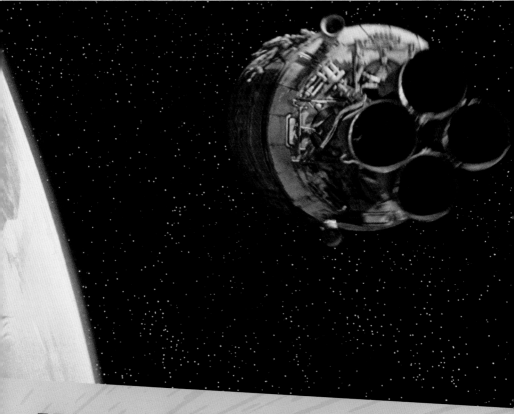

How does R2-D2 escape the Empire?

In an escape pod! R2-D2 and C-3PO **eject** themselves into space in this **small vehicle** during an important mission. The Empire is trying to find them and **capture** them, but R2-D2 won't let that stop him.

What is a hologram?

A special type of picture. Droids use computer **technology** and **blue light** to project holograms. They can be used to send **messages** or to help people **communicate** with one another.

What message does Princess Leia give R2-D2?

A secret one! Leia **records** a special hologram message for Jedi Obi-Wan Kenobi. It is R2-D2's job to **play** Obi-Wan this message. Leia appears in the picture, as if she was really there!

What else can R2-D2 project?

Maps! R2-D2's rebel friends often ask him to show them hologram maps of the **whole galaxy.** Then they can see where their enemies are, or how to travel to **faraway planets.**

Who wants to sell R2-D2?

Jawas! These creatures are **scavengers.** They gather up and sell all sorts of scrap for money. They also **sell droids!** They think someone on their planet Tatooine will **buy** R2-D2.

Where does R2-D2 meet Luke?

On Tatooine. Luke works on a moisture farm on this sandy planet. When he needs new droids to **help him** on the farm, he thinks R2-D2 looks **useful.** He's not wrong!

Can R2-D2 find his friends?

Of course! When R2-D2 **loses** his rebel friends he uses his computer skills to **find** them. They've fallen into a trash compactor! He stops them from being **squashed,** then breaks down the door to free them!

When was R2-D2 scared?

When his friend Luke went missing on the snowy planet Hoth. There the snow was so **deep** that R2-D2 could not go out looking for him. He had to use his **sensors** to hunt for his friend.

an R2-D2 swim?

ort of! On a mission to Dagobah, R2-D2 falls nto a **swamp.** His circuits are shielded against water damage, and he is able to **float** his way out of danger.

as R2-D2 ever been captured?

Sadly, yes. Poor R2-D2 becomes the prisoner of slug-like **gangster Jabba the Hutt**. He is used as a **drink cart!** However, R2-D2 is soon able to escape. Clever droid!

What does R2-D2 hide for Luke?

His lightsaber! R2-D2's chest contains secret compartments. They are perfectly sized for storing Luke's weapon. When Luke is in trouble, R2-D2 launches his lightsaber toward him. **Catch,** Luke!

Has R2-D2 ever been used in a test?

Strangely, yes.

On the swampy planet Dagobah, R2-D2 is surprised to become part of some **Jedi training.** Old Jedi Master Yoda challenges Luke Skywalker to use the power of **the Force** to make R2-D2 **levitate!**

What is the Force?

A powerful energy. The Force exists in all **living things.** Jedi learn how to use it **for good.** As a droid, R2-D2 cannot use the Force.

Has R2-D2 ever been given an award?

Yes. After a big battle, the rebels succeed in destroying a key weapon belonging to the Empire. R2-D2 takes part in the **victory celebrations.** The rebel leaders recognize the important part he played in helping them **win.**

How does R2-D2 cope with sand?

With difficulty! R2-D2's **feet** are made of **treads** and **little wheels.** These treads are designed for **all terrains,** but rolling across sand dunes is hard work! **Keep rolling,** R2-D2!

Does R2-D2 like the cold?

Not really. If it's snowing a **blizzard,** even R2-D2 struggles to see. And a big **gust** of **wind** could make this little droid **topple over!** On frozen planets such as Hoth it's safer for R2-D2 to stay indoors.

Has R2-D2 visited forests?

He has. On the forest moon of Endor, R2-D2 finds himself traveling up into the **treetops!** R2-D2 is not scared of heights, and thinks the forest is pretty. But he prefers to be back on **solid ground.**

What happens when R2-D2 meets the Ewoks?

He is very quickly surrounded!

These furry creatures want to protect their homeworld. They think that R2-D2's friends are a **threat,** so they tie them all up. Plucky R2-D2 **cuts** his friends **free** with his tools!

Does R2-D2 ever run out of power?

Yes. R2-D2 is sad when his good friend and master Luke Skywalker goes **missing,** so he turns himself off. Everyone **gives up** trying to fix him. Thankfully he wakes up all by himself!

Finn

Rey